THIS BOOK BELONGS TO

Matthew 5:16

Let your light so shine before men,
that they may see your good works and
glorify your Father which is in heaven.

This book is dedicated
to all the orphans
in the world

Once upon a time in a small village far away, there was a poor young girl named Tatiana. Her classmates called her Tatty because her clothes, although clean, were old and tattered. She had no friends because she kept to herself a lot. She walked to and from school all by herself.

Many nights she would cry herself to sleep because she thought nobody liked her. This made her very sad.

Coming home one day, she bumped into a boy named Simon from her school. They made eye contact, and Simon smiled slightly even though he thought Tatty was a bit weird. She ran off to her house smiling and thinking, Oh, Simon likes me!

The following school day, everyone was making fun of her. The girls at school knew she liked Simon. Tatiana was so embarrassed.

Very early next morning, Tatiana decided to skip school and take a walk into the woods. She trudged along a path on the outskirts of her village for what seemed like miles, not knowing where to go. She plopped down on the side of the road to rest and covered her face with her hands.

Hearing a sound, Tatiana looked up and saw an old lady. She was rather tattered and worn. In the sweetest voice the old woman asked, "Where are you off to my dear?" Tatiana looked up to the heavens and said, "Any place but here!" Then she started sobbing. The old woman handed her a beautiful, embroidered handkerchief and said, "Wipe your tears my child, everything will be alright. Come sit at my campfire and have a rest."

While Tatiana rested, the old woman hummed as she busied herself making up some soup over the campfire.

To Tatiana's amazement, she noticed that the birds, rabbits, and other small animals were gathering around them. The kind old woman tossed bits of bread to these small beautiful creatures and they rushed the food like it was a game. She even spoke to the animals and it seemed like they understood each other.

The old woman gave Tatiana a battered tin cup filled with steaming chicken broth. The taste of the broth, nature's harmony around her, and the kindness of the woman made Tatiana feel like she was in heaven. She felt at peace and never wanted the day to be over. Tatiana couldn't have asked for a better place to be.

The old woman smiled at Tatiana with the kindest eyes and then spoke words of wisdom. "Little child, you have a whole life ahead of you. Jesus loves you. He wants you to know that so that you can love yourself and be more confident. You see, these stars are millions of miles away but we can still see their beauty. No one can put that light out. Let your light shine and others will see it. Don't let anyone put your light out. Anytime you feel down ask Jesus to fill you up with his Holy Spirit. His Holy Spirit will give you wisdom and fill you up with Joy.

Tatiana turned to the old woman and wiped her tears again on the handkerchief. She smiled at the old woman and gave her a hug. It was starting to get dark. The old woman said, "Perhaps it's time for you to go home now. Your family will be worried about you." Tatiana nodded and said, "Okay, I'll go back." The old woman walked Tatiana to the edge of the village and bade her goodbye.

It was a long walk for Tatty. When she got home, to her amazement, Simon and some of her classmates were in front of her house with her mother. They had missed her at school and they were all planning to go search for her. They were so happy to see her. Simon was the first person to walk up to her. Tatiana cried tears of joy. She told them how she had felt and why she had run away. They hugged her and promised to be her friend.

From that time on, Tatiana felt more confident in herself. She smiled and said "Hello" as she passed people and they smiled back. She played happily with her friends at school.

A few days later, Tatiana went back to look for the kind old woman. When she got to the campsite, there was no trace of the old woman or her belongings, not even any ashes from the campfire.

Tatiana was puzzled. As she was about to leave, she looked down at her feet. There, she saw the same embroidered handkerchief that the kind old woman had given her. Stitched on it were the words...

JUST BE YOU
SHINE LIKE THE STARS

ABOUT THE AUTHOR

Ngozi Elizabeth Mbonu was born in Ottawa, and eventually relocated to Toronto, Ontario because she fell in love with the city and culture. Since childhood, writing has always been a passion of hers. She hopes Shine! will inspire and encourage young boys and girls to know that God has put so much talents and abilities in them and they need to let the light inside of them Shine so bright. Everybody is unique and God wants you to be confident knowing that he loves you Elizabeth would like to thank God for her wonderful and supportive parents, my lovely brothers , Julie Thomas for editing the story, Dipa for illustrating this book, as well as friends and family for all their support.